# Walt Disney's

## Lady and the TRAMP

Illustrated by the Disney Storybook Artists
Adapted by Kate Hannigan

© Disney Enterprises, Inc.
Visit our Web site at www.disneybooks.com

Published by
Louis Weber, C.E.O.
Publications International, Ltd.
7373 North Cicero Avenue
Lincolnwood, Illinois 60712

**www.pilbooks.com**

Manufactured in China.

8 7 6 5 4 3 2 1

ISBN: 0-7853-9541-5

In a cozy house on a tree-lined street, there lived a beautiful puppy with big eyes and honey-brown hair. Her name was Lady, and she was a happy dog. She lived with two kind humans, Jim Dear and Darling.

Lady started every morning the same way. She stretched her legs and hopped down from Jim Dear and Darling's billowy bed. Then she ran outside to chase the birds and fetch the newspaper.

Jim Dear and Darling loved Lady. They enjoyed little more than playing with Lady and watching her grow from a puppy into an adult dog.

One day, they had a surprise. Since she was getting to be such a big girl, and because they loved her so much, Jim Dear and Darling gave Lady a shiny new license and a fancy dog collar.

Lady was very proud of her new collar. She thought she looked quite pretty in it. She ran outside to show her best friends, Jock and Trusty.

The collar wasn't her only news. Lady also learned that Jim Dear and Darling were going to have a baby.

At first Lady thought it was good news. She was very proud of her family. But soon Lady made a new friend who warned her not to get too excited about a new baby.

Lady's new friend was a dog named Tramp. He was a happy-go-lucky dog with scruffy fur, a twinkle in his eyes, and a sly smile.

Tramp had a good life, but it was very different from Lady's. He didn't live with a family who loved him, and he didn't have a yard full of birds to chase. Tramp did whatever he wanted and went wherever he pleased. Some days he ate at the bakery, and other days he visited the Italian restaurant. He always stayed one step ahead of the dogcatcher and made sure his friends did, too.

Tramp spent his days wandering all around town. And that's how, one day, he wandered into Lady's yard.

Tramp couldn't believe what a beauty Lady was! He walked right into the yard and joined her as she talked with Jock and Trusty about her fancy new collar and the fancy new baby that was coming.

Tramp shook his scruffy head.

"When the baby moves in," Tramp warned Lady, "the dog moves out!"

"Really?" Lady asked with a little gulp. "Are you sure?"

"Trust me, Lady," Tramp said. "I'm sure. It's a sad, sad story that I know too, too well."

The dogs were all worried. Lady didn't know how to live without a family to take care of her.

When the baby finally did arrive, it wasn't so bad. Jim
Dear was breathless with excitement. Darling was so
happy, she was singing and humming all the time.

Lady still wasn't quite sure what a baby was.

Jim Dear helped her peek into the cradle, and Lady fell
in love. Now she had three humans to care for, and three
humans to care for her!

Before too long, Jim Dear and Darling had to take a
trip. They weren't planning on taking the baby with them.

"How could they leave this sweet baby?" Lady thought.

"You didn't think we'd just leave the baby here on its own, did you?" Jim Dear asked her. He assured Lady that someone was coming to help take care of the baby.

That someone was Aunt Sarah.

Lady wagged her tail and proudly led Aunt Sarah in to see the baby. Lady was confident that she could show Aunt Sarah just what to do.

But Aunt Sarah wanted nothing to do with Lady.

Aunt Sarah liked cats. In particular, she liked her cats, and she brought them along with her to Lady's house.

They were nothing but trouble! From the minute they arrived, the Siamese cats were up to no good, knocking over vases, tipping over the fishbowl, and making a mess of things.

Lady barked and barked, trying to control them. But Aunt Sarah didn't understand.

"I want a good, strong muzzle," Aunt Sarah told the man at the pet store.

A muzzle? Lady couldn't bear it! She ran as fast as she could to get away from it — and from Aunt Sarah!

Lady ran out of the store and down the street. She dashed through traffic and was almost run over!

A pack of dogs began to chase Lady. They had mean faces and loud barks. Lady was so frightened that she didn't know what to do.

"Leave her alone!" shouted Tramp. He jumped in front of the ferocious dogs and chased them away.

Tramp saved Lady's life.

Lady was scared. She was breathing hard, her heart was racing, and she was embarrassed about the muzzle.

"We've got to get this thing off you," Tramp said.

He took Lady to the zoo. Maybe one of their animal friends could help.

They walked past the apes and alligators and a laughing hyena. None of them could help Lady.

Then they saw a busy beaver. Tramp started talking and talking. The next thing Lady knew, the beaver bit right through the leather strap!

The muzzle was off. What a relief, thought Lady. Thank goodness for Tramp!

It was time to celebrate.

Lady and Tramp walked all around town. Tramp showed her his favorite places to stop for a meal. Best of all was Tony's Italian Restaurant.

"No bones for you tonight," Tony said after seeing Lady with Tramp. "Tonight is special! Spaghetti and meatballs!"

Tony set the table with a fancy tablecloth and a candle. He served them dinner on a plate! He even played the accordion and sang love songs.

As they slurped their romantic spaghetti dinner, Lady
and Tramp fell in love.

After a moonlit walk through the park, Lady and Tramp
went to sleep. In the morning, Lady awoke with a start.

"I have to get home to take care of the baby!" she said.

Tramp walked Lady home, but on the way he wanted to have some fun. "Let's chase some chickens!" he said.

Feathers flew as the dogs chased the birds all around the yard. Just as Lady and Tramp slipped through a fence to leave, the dogcatcher appeared!

Tramp ran ahead, laughing about their silly game. When he turned around to talk to Lady, she was gone.

The dogcatcher had caught Lady! She was on her way to the pound.

Luckily Lady wore her collar and shiny license. Before long, the dogcatcher let her go home — but not before Lady heard all sorts of stories about Tramp, and the trouble he liked to get into, from the other dogs.

Once Lady returned home, Tramp stopped by to apologize. "I'm sorry, Pidge," he said. Tramp called her Pidge or Pigeon when he wanted to be sweet.

Lady was too angry to speak to Tramp. She was tied to a long chain and had to sleep in the doghouse.

As the rain poured down, Lady was miserable.

In the darkness of the yard, she saw something move. It was a rat!

Lady barked wildly and ran toward it, but the chain caught her. She couldn't stop the rat!

Tramp ran back into the yard.

"What is it, Pigeon?" he asked.

Lady told him she saw the rat scurry into the house.

Tramp sneaked inside and chased the rat. Lady broke
free from the chain and ran to help him. The rat was in
the baby's room!

The dogs barked wildly as they fought the rat. Finally,
they got it.

"I must call the pound!" Aunt Sarah screamed as she
found Lady and Tramp in the baby's room.

The dogcatcher came and took Tramp away.

Jim Dear and Darling were returning home as the
dogcatcher locked up Tramp in the wagon.

"It's just a stray dog," the dogcatcher said. "A real troublemaker. Caught him attacking your baby."

Jim Dear and Darling ran up to the baby's room. The baby was sleeping soundly. Lady pointed toward the rat.

"Lady, I think you and your friend were trying to save our baby from this rat!" Jim Dear said.

Lady's friends Jock and Trusty chased the dogcatcher's wagon. Tramp was a good friend. They had to save him!

When the friends finally caught up to the dogcatcher,
Trusty barked at the wagon. The horses reared up in
fright, and the wagon tipped over.

Lady and Jim Dear jumped into his car and chased the
dogcatcher, too. They rescued Tramp just in time!

They heard Jock howling into the night air. He was sad
for his best friend Trusty. He thought Trusty was hurt, but
everything turned out okay. Trusty had broken his leg, but
he had also helped to save Tramp's life.

Before long, Jim Dear and Darling's house grew busier. There was the *pitter pat* of little human feet, as well as the pounding of puppy paws.

Tramp had come to settle down with Lady. And they had given birth to four wonderful puppies — three who looked like Lady, and one who looked just like Tramp!

The puppies grew up in a home filled with love. Not only did they have their parents and their humans. Lady and Tramp's puppies also had the best uncles a dog could ask for in Jock and Trusty.